BUTTERFLIES KEEP FLYING

By Ali Pfautz Illustrated by Sara Grier

Published by

Artistic Endeavors
Press

Ali Pfautz
thestoryladyva.com

ISBN 978-0-9916527-3-0 (paperback)

For Ella,
Keep flying my sweet beauty!

With great thanks and love to my Dad,
a passionate educator and amazing human,
who always taught me . . .
people are the most important thing!
— A.P.

To Catherine, Mike, JP, and Louie,
I'm continually amazed by your capacity for love and caring,
and your ability to keep flying despite life's great challenges.
You all are inspirations!
— S.G.

A NOTE FROM THE AUTHOR

Butterfly children is the name given to boys and girls who suffer from a rare and very painful skin disease called Epidermolysis Bullosa, or EB. These children have skin that's as fragile as a butterfly's wings. My friend Ella battles EB every day. She is the butterfly child whose brave spirit and gentle soul inspired this story.

Sometimes I imagine I'm an elephant . . .

. . . with a huge body that shakes the houses in my neighborhood as I walk to school.

During recess, I could let my friends climb up my dangly tail and slide down my super sturdy trunk.

WHEEE!

Sometimes I imagine I'm a giraffe . . .

... with skinny legs, a spotty body, and a leeeeeeeeoong neck.

Every day I could easily stretch
myself high up in the sky and disappear
into fluffy, cotton candy clouds.

I'd spend hours hiding up there,
munching on all of that sticky goodness.

YUM! YUM!

Sometimes I imagine I'm a lion...

. . . with a shaggy head of hair and a regal tail. I would be a king and always wear my jeweled crown.

I'd get lots of attention
because of my booming roar,
the loudest in all the land.

But I'm not strong like an elephant.

I am a butterfly . . .
with a tiny body and colorful,
fragile wings.

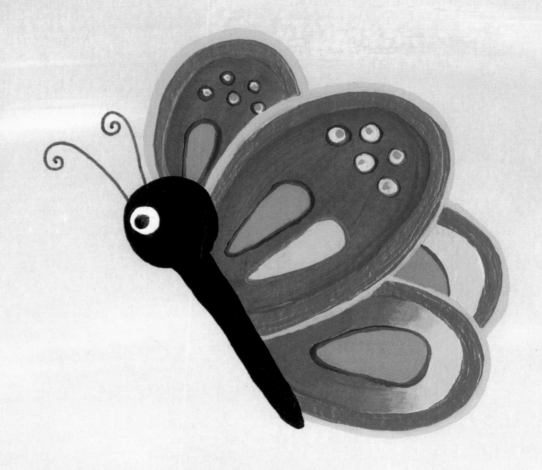

Butterflies begin life as fuzzy caterpillars
crunching on leaves all day long.

Then slowly,
our bodies change
into graceful,
winged creatures.

Butterflies spend each day diving in and out of brilliant seas of petals.

We flutter in search of tall flowers, small flowers, bright bubbly flowers.

The blossoms feed us and love us.

Then we fly away, carrying that love, and spreading it around to help make more flowers.

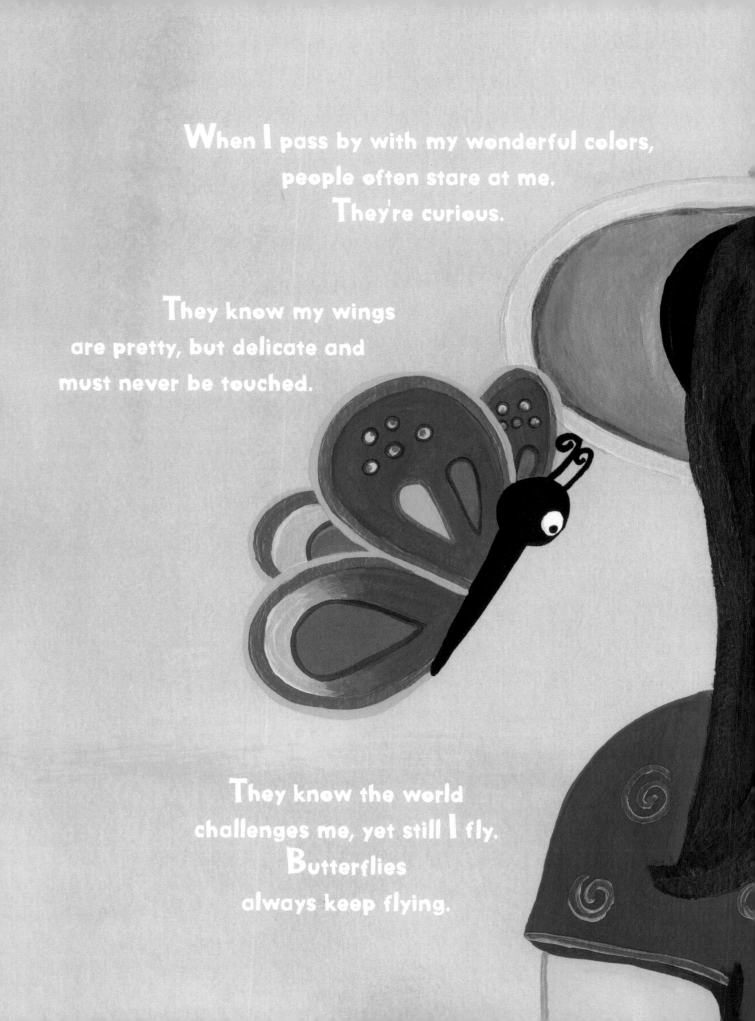

When I pass by with my wonderful colors,
people often stare at me.
They're curious.

They know my wings
are pretty, but delicate and
must never be touched.

They know the world
challenges me, yet still I fly.
Butterflies
always keep flying.

When the air becomes crisp and cold,
the only way for a butterfly to stay warm is to flap its wings.

So we keep flying to heat up our bodies.

When droopy raindrops t u m b l e from the sky, it hurts our sensitive wings.

We keep flying to find shelter that will protect us.

When the wind blows, it bounces our bodies around,

confusing us, and changing our direction.

We must keep flying to discover a different way.

Sometimes I get tired of flying. That's when I imagine being some other amazing creature . . .

. . . one without these
beautiful,
breakable wings.

Then, the sun rises on a new day.
Its warmth fills the world with

possibility.

I soar into the air once again, because . . .

I am a butterfly . . .

small and fragile,
yet **STRONG**.
And butterflies keep flying.

A BUTTERFLY CHILD

My buddy Ella flies gracefully through life while facing many challenges. She has a disease called Epidermolysis Bullosa, or EB. Ella and others with EB are called the butterfly children because their skin is as delicate as a butterfly's wings. Even a quick touch, like a tight hug, can cause painful tears and blisters on their bodies. For Ella, there are days she can't go out for recess, the sun and the rough movements hurt her skin. Sometimes she can't eat the foods she wants because her throat and stomach are sensitive, too. Her life doesn't always follow the path of a "typical" little girl, but Ella keeps flying.

SOME FACTS ABOUT EB*

- One in 20,000 children are born with EB each year.

- Every day many children with EB must bandage parts of their bodies—tummy, legs, arms—to protect their wounds from infection.

- The bandages EB children need can cost as much as $10,000 a month.

If you purchased this book, a portion of those funds went directly to debra of America, a nonprofit group dedicated to research and services for EB families. For more information, please visit **debra.org.**

Thank you!

*Source: Dystrophic Epidermolysis Bullosa Research Association of America (debra of America)

A GREAT BIG THANK YOU!!

You are holding this book in your hands because
of the generosity of 70 people who donated to
our BUTTERFLY CHILD Kickstarter campaign.
The people listed on the next page donated $100 or more.
We are so grateful, and our heartfelt thanks go out to
all of our supporters! For a complete list of our Kickstarter
donors visit Ali's website, **thestoryladyva.com**.

THANK YOU!!

Sharon Freeland Harris, DMD, PC

Lindy McHutchison

Elizabeth and William McGuire

Jennifer Kingman

Georgia Ramirez

Michael Pfautz

Rene and Ron Rickabaugh

Gale and Ron Alexander

The McCaughey Family

Carol Schultheis

Chris Hobbs

Mike Policicchio

Roy and Charlotte Grier

Michael & Ebba Stedillie

Ms. A. L. Britt

Carter & Caroline Walker

Jo Ann Shibley

Andrew Cantella

Patrick Gregory Miller

Joe and Brenda Simpson

Jennifer Eckert

Ellen Peacock

Beth Anne Pretty

With her polka dot pants and an array of goofy hats, children's storyteller, Ali Pfautz, entertains kids of all ages. Known as The Story Lady, she gets everyone involved with her tales and songs. The audience might become characters, sound effects, or sometimes, she just really needs somebody to be a tree. Ali teaches dance and theater classes as well as preschool music and movement.

Ali is the author of **No More Slooping, Sara Sue!** and the poetry book, **Smiles and Wiggles: A Year of Imaginative Fun.** She believes in the power of a smile. When she's not telling stories and singing songs, Ali is smiling and laughing in Richmond, VA with her two daughters, her husband, and their furry sidekick, Bear.

Visit Ali online at **thestoryladyva.com** or "like" her at **facebook.com/AliPfautzTheStoryLady**.

Sara Grier is an artist whose heart leaps at the opportunity to spread joy through color and imagery. Sara discovered her love of art at a young age and went on to earn a BA in fine art from Elon University. That's where she discovered her passion for paint. She often experiments with the varied tones of watercolors and acrylics. A lover of children's books, Sara tapped into her inner child in recent years, painting characters for the poetry compilation, **Smiles and Wiggles: A Year of Imaginative Fun**, by Ali Pfautz. Sara and Ali teamed up again for **Butterflies Keep Flying**.

Sara lives in Midlothian, VA with her wild bunch, two sons and a daughter. You can find Sara online at **facebook.com/ artistSaraGrier.**

Made in the USA
Lexington, KY
12 September 2016